P9-CMT-694

FREDERICK COUNTY PUBLIC LIBRARIES

TOWN MOUSE COUNTRY MOUSE

JAN BRETT

G. P. PUTNAM'S SONS
NEW YORK

Copyright © 1994 by Jan Brett
All rights reserved. This book, or parts thereof, may not be reproduced
in any form without permission in writing from the publisher.
G. P. Putnam's Sons, a division of The Putnam & Grosset Group,
345 Hudson Street, New York, NY 10014.
G. P. Putnam's Sons, Reg. U.S. Pat. & Tm. Off.
Published simultaneously in Canada.
Manufactured in China by RR Donnelley Asia Printing Solutions Ltd.
Airbrush backgrounds by Joseph Hearne.
Book designed by Nanette Stevenson.
Lettering by Dave Gatti. Text set in Bembo.

Library of Congress Cataloging-in-Publication Data
Brett, Jan, 1949- Town mouse, country mouse / Jan Brett. p. cm.
Summary: After trading houses, the country mice and
the town mice discover there's no place like home.
[1. Fables. 2. Mice—Folklore.] I. Title. PZ8.2.B6675To
1994 398.24'5293233—dc20 93-41227 CIP AC

ISBN 978-0-399-22622-9

For my niece,
Sophie Tsairis

One morning, the town mouse woke up shivering from a dream about the kitchen cat who prowled the house. "I need a vacation," he said to his wife. "Let me take you to see the countryside where I was born. Life is quiet and peaceful there. The sun shines brightly every day, and the air is so clear that you can see the stars at night. And nothing will prepare you for the taste of wild blackberries." "Let's go right away!" she said. So the town mouse and his wife packed a picnic and set off for the country.

The country mouse and her husband were at their tree-stump house, exhausted from searching for food and avoiding the hungry owl who lived nearby. "Sometimes I wish we lived in a town house where all the food you can eat is right there in the pantry. They say that the smell of cheese makes your whiskers tingle." "Mine are tingling already," her husband exclaimed.

The town mice were outside the country mice's house putting a huge chunk of cheese in the middle of their picnic cloth. The country mice peered down at it. They heard the town mouse exclaim: "This is the life! Wildflowers, spring peepers. If only we lived here!" The country mice crept out. "You like it here?" they asked. "Why, we've always wanted to live in a town house." The town mouse offered them a nibble of cheese. "Why don't we trade houses?" he said. "Would you?" asked the country mouse, her mouth stuffed full of the delicious cheese. "We'll leave right away," she said. As they said good-bye, each of the mice thought that they had the better part of the bargain.

It was dark when the country mice arrived in town and found the house. They tiptoed inside and wandered into the sewing room where they found what they thought was a sumptuous bed and fell sound asleep. Much too early the next morning, a loud clanging woke them up. Sooty clouds of smoke were pouring over them and they heard a strange voice purring loudly: "Sauces and ham, it's hungry I am! Sauces and ham, it's hungry I am. Mice in my stew, wait till I catch you!" "Who do you think *that* is?" the country mouse asked his wife.

The town mouse and his wife were up with the birds, ready to gather wild blackberries in the grassy meadow for breakfast. They could smell them. They just couldn't find them. As the town mouse's wife turned to remind her husband to remember the way home, she felt a large wet drop on her head. "What was that?" she asked. "Is the bathtub leaking?" "No, we're in the country now," he said. "Those are raindrops." Just then, lightning lit up the sky, and rain poured down as the two drenched mice ran wildly for their tree-stump home.

OLIV

The country mice were looking forward to their first splendid meal in the pantry. "I'm sure there is ham in the ice chest and rolls in the bread box. But the best smell of all is coming from up there," the country mouse told her husband. "It must be a fine old cheese. I'll climb on your shoulders and get it." But she couldn't quite reach it. "Stand on your toes," she called down. But just as she got ahold of the cheese, her husband lost his balance. The top slammed down, and she was left hanging by her tail. "Help me! Help me! I'm caught."

Back in the country, the town mouse had put on dry clothes. He was especially proud of his bright new jacket. "So colorful and eye-catching," he said to his wife. "Let's stroll in the forest. We'll come back loaded with acorns and hickory nuts." But their walk was soon interrupted. The town mouse's colorful coat was so eye-catching that it caught the eye of a curious black bird, and if his wife hadn't held him by his foot, he would have been carried off.

Not far away in town, the country mouse felt his wife's silky tail. "Nothing broken," he said. But when he looked in her eyes, he saw how sad and discouraged she was. "I know something that will cheer us up," he told her. "Follow me." He had spied a small window up above the pantry shelves. Together they climbed higher and higher. When they reached the top, he rubbed away the soot, and they looked out at a piece of blue sky. "Doesn't it look like home?" the country mouse asked his wife.

The town mice stood quietly together after their awful black bird scare. "I thought I had lost you forever," the town mouse whispered to her husband. They looked around. How still and peaceful it was now. The sun had come out, and everything was glistening and green. "It is beautiful here," she said. "We should try to enjoy it." "I know," the town mouse said. "But I miss the sound of the town—all the hustle and bustle. Here I feel so alone." "And in our cozy town house, we knew what to expect," his wife added.

HONG KONG
1.50 S
REPUBLIK OSTERREICH
50
NIPPON
29 USA
POSTA ROMANA
ARTA POPULARA
1 L
POSTA ROMANA
1.80
ONE NATION INDIVISIBLE · E PLURIBUS UNUM
USA 13c
4 Ft
MAGYAR POSTA
PRIVATPOST
SVERIGE 1.80

The country mice knew to stay at home in a thunderstorm, and they knew what to expect from the hungry owl. But they soon found out that there were different dangers here when they discovered a tasty morsel of blue cheese sitting on a pine board. "This time *you* take the cheese. I'm still shaking from being caught in the cheese box," the country mouse said. So her husband crept toward the cheese, whiskers trembling. As he reached it, his foot slipped, and he heard a *whoosh*, followed by an enormous snap, and he was thrown across the room. He landed in a warm bundle of something soft and furry.

The country mouse was shaking from his close call. "I can barely stand." He winced as his wife pulled him up and patted down his crumpled whiskers. It was then that she noticed the bundle on which her husband had landed was tipping and turning. It was alive! Two green eyes snapped open. "Run!" she cried, getting a good look at it. "It's an owl with teeth!"

UNITED STATES OF AMERICA
ONE DOLLAR
50
CENTS
ONE PENNY

The town mice knew how to avoid mousetraps set with cheese, but they soon found that the country has its own perils when they explored the riverbank, hand in hand. Suddenly the water began to boil and churn and a huge wet head popped up and stared at them. It was a river otter. The mice tore back to their tree-stump home, only to find a hedgehog rolled into a ball in front of the door. Then they heard an animal crashing toward them through the underbrush. "I can't take this anymore!" the town mouse quaked, and she raced for the nearest tree with her husband right behind her.

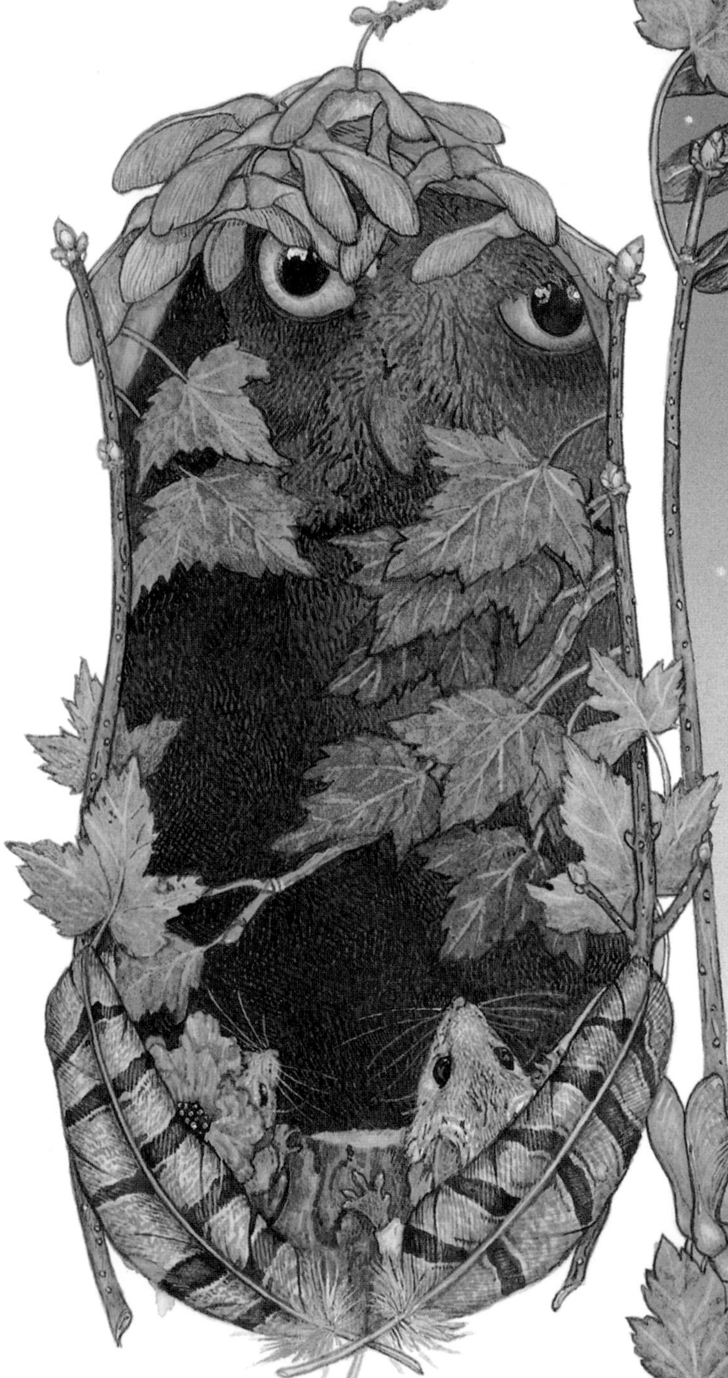

From the tree, they could see the town lights blink on as the sun went down and the stars came out one by one. "What shall we do?" the town mouse asked his wife. But before she could answer, she saw a pair of glowering eyes right beside them and they were face to face with the most terrifying creature of all. "A cat with wings!" shrieked the town mouse. "That's it for me!" his wife cried, and they ran down the tree and toward the town as fast as their legs could take them.

As the town mice headed frantically along the road, the country mice were fleeing in terror toward the country. Their paths crossed, but neither saw the other, they were so frightened. Even the sky seemed to be falling down on them! The country mice didn't stop running until they could see their tree stump in the distance.

The town mice kept on running until they reached their town house. The musty smell of old wood, and smoke from the kitchen, all seemed wonderful. Even the street sounds outside sounded cheerful and friendly. "There's no place like home," sighed the town mouse, as he and his wife settled into a warm old slipper. "There's no place like home."

Atop their cozy tree-stump house, the country mouse and her husband looked up at a full moon shining down on them. They sighed happily. "We missed you," they said together.

Back on the road, the cat and owl had knocked each other out when they collided head-on. The cat, slowly waking up, touched his bruised head gingerly. He looked up to see the owl brushing himself off. It was then that he had an idea. "Owl, how would you like to trade places with me? I've always wanted to try the simple life in the country!"